For John, the best editor in the Milky Way

SIMON & SCHUSTER BOOKS FOR YOUNG READERS
Simon & Schuster Building, Rockefeller Center
1230 Avenue of the Americas, New York, New York 10020
Text copyright © 1994 by Marilyn Sadler
Illustrations copyright © 1994 by Roger Bollen

SIMON & SCHUSTER BOOKS FOR YOUNG READERS
is a trademark of Simon & Schuster.
The text of this book is set in 14 point Futura Medium.
The illustrations were done in mixed media.
Manufactured in the United States of America

10 9 8 7 6 5 4 3 2

Library of Congress Cataloging-in-Publication Data
Sadler, Marilyn. Alistair and the alien invasion / by
Marilyn Sadler; illustrated by Roger Bollen.
p. cm. Summary: When aliens invade from outer space,
boy genius Alistair is the only person able to save the Earth.
[1. Extraterrestrial beings—Fiction.] I. Bollen, Roger, ill.
II. Title. PZ7.S1239Aj 1994 [E]—dc20 92-22828
CIP ISBN: 0-671-75957-4

ALISTAIR AND THE ALIEN INVASION

By Marilyn Sadler
Illustrated by Roger Bollen

SIMON & SCHUSTER BOOKS FOR YOUNG READERS
Published by Simon & Schuster
New York   London   Toronto   Sydney   Tokyo   Singapore

Alistair Grittle was a most unusual boy. There was no one else quite like him.

He was very well-dressed. Every morning he pressed his shirt and his jacket as well as his socks and his shoelaces.

He was polite and well-mannered. He never left school without thanking Mr. Fudwinkle for giving him homework.

He was also a boy genius. He read his first set of encyclopedias when he was three years old.

He won his first Annual Twickadilly Science Competition with his formula for invisibility at the age of five.

He was just about to tell them one of their taillights was out when, all of a sudden, they shot a large beam of light at Earth.

Alistair was rounding the turn at Venus, making very good time through the Milky Way, when he saw a space ship filled with aliens heading toward Earth.

And by the time he was eight, he had already been to the moon and back in a space ship he built in his basement. There was no question about it. Alistair was not an ordinary boy.

Then one day, Mr. Fudwinkle gave Alistair's class quite an interesting science project.

"I want you to bring in the most unusual plant you can find," he said.

So Alistair did what any boy genius would do.

He got into his space ship and set out to find the most unusual plant in the universe.

Alistair was a bit concerned, so he turned his ship around. When he got home, he was not surprised to find all the people of Twickadilly floating upside down in the sky. It was just as he suspected.

Earth was being invaded by aliens.

Alistair did not have time for an alien invasion. He was in the middle of a science project. But he knew that he could not let the aliens take over Earth. So he made himself invisible and went to spy on them.

When Alistair found the aliens, they were beaming up plants of every kind into their space ships. It was unlike any alien invasion Alistair had ever seen.

Alistair was quite curious about the aliens. So he
threw himself into a beam of light and went aboard
one of the ships with a couple of petunias.

Once on board, Alistair found the aliens studying all of
the plants they had taken. He was very pleased to see
they were organizing and naming them.

The aliens were in the middle of studying some
crabgrass when, all of a sudden, Alistair's formula for
invisibility wore off, and Alistair became visible again.
The aliens thought Alistair was the most unusual
Earthling they had ever seen. He was far more
interesting than plant life.

The aliens wanted to know everything about Alistair.
So they invited themselves to his house. On the way
home, Alistair spotted a few of his classmates. He could
see they had already found their plants.

When Alistair got home, he introduced the aliens to his parents. The aliens asked Alistair's parents many questions about Alistair.

The more the aliens learned about Alistair, the more they wanted to know. They were delighted when they discovered the Grittle family photo album. Every time they came to a picture of Alistair, they asked if they could keep it.

The aliens spent most of that day and evening in Alistair's room. They fed his octopus. They licked stamps for his stamp collection. They even tried a few of his chemistry experiments.

Soon it was late, and Alistair was tired. He hoped the
aliens would leave, but the aliens did not want to leave.
They wanted to sleep in Alistair's bed.

The next morning Alistair got up quietly.
He wanted to leave for outer space to
search for his plant without the aliens.
But the aliens heard his steam iron
and woke up.

The aliens had other plans that morning. They wanted to see Alistair's school, but school was closed. The aliens were very disappointed. They had wanted more than anything to go through Alistair's desk.

As they returned to their space ship, the phone rang.
The aliens were sorry they hadn't turned on their
answering machine.

It was their leader calling. He was wondering what was taking them so long on Earth. They were supposed to be on Gootula by now.

The aliens did not want to go to Gootula. They were having too much fun with Alistair. But they could not be impolite to their leader. So it was agreed they must move on.

Before the aliens left, Alistair asked them to bring everyone down from the sky. "Science projects due today!" said Mr. Fudwinkle as he touched the ground.

Alistair did not know what to do. He had not even begun to look for his plant. It was going to be the first time in his life he was late with his homework.

Then, to Alistair's surprise, the aliens gave him a present. "We found it on the planet Balooloo," they said. "It's a Kadoodle, the most unusual plant in the universe." Alistair was very happy. He had not realized how well-mannered the aliens were.

When it was time for the aliens to leave, they hugged Alistair goodbye. Alistair could hear them crying inside their space suits.

Then the aliens left Earth.

It was a great day for everyone in Twickadilly.
Alistair finished his science project on time.
Mr. Fudwinkle loved the Kadoodle from
Balooloo. And Earth had been saved from an
alien invasion.

No one was surprised, however, that Alistair had saved
Earth. After all, he was a most unusual boy. There was
certainly no one else quite like him...

...in the entire universe.